The Baby Is Here!

adapted by Angela C. Santomero

based on the screenplays "Daniel Learns About Being a Big Brother" written by

Angela C. Santomero and "The Baby is Here"

written by Angela C. Santomero and Becky Friedman

poses and layouts by Jason Fruchter

Simon Spotlight

New York   London   Toronto   Sydney   New Delhi

SIMON SPOTLIGHT
An imprint of Simon & Schuster Children's Publishing Division
1230 Avenue of the Americas, New York, New York 10020
First Simon Spotlight edition January 2015
© 2015 The Fred Rogers Company
All rights reserved, including the right of reproduction in whole or in part in any form.
SIMON SPOTLIGHT and colophon are registered trademarks of Simon & Schuster, Inc.
For information about special discounts for bulk purchases, please contact Simon & Schuster
Special Sales at 1-866-506-1949 or business@simonandschuster.com.
Manufactured in the United States of America 0915 LAK
10 9 8 7 6 5
ISBN 978-1-4814-3013-5
ISBN 978-1-4814-3014-2 (eBook)

It's a beautiful day in the neighborhood, and Daniel Tiger is very excited. "Today is a special day," says Daniel. "Mom is going to have a baby!"

Everyone has lots to do to get ready for the new baby. Daniel helps Mom and Dad get the baby's room ready.

"*You can be a big helper in your family,*" Dad Tiger sings.

Daniel helps Dad paint the new baby's room.

Daniel helps Mom unpack his old baby clothes. Daniel can't believe he used to be little enough to wear this teeny-tiny sweater!

Then Daniel helps Dad push his old crib into the room for the new baby.

The baby's room is ready! But Daniel wants to do one more thing.

"The baby's room needs a picture of our family," Daniel says. First he draws a picture of himself. Next he draws the new baby. Then he adds Mom and Dad Tiger.

"Our family!" Daniel says.

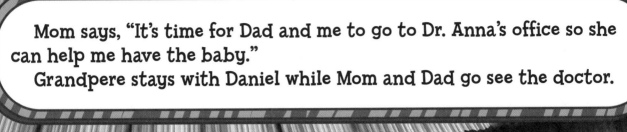

Mom says, "It's time for Dad and me to go to Dr. Anna's office so she can help me have the baby."
Grandpere stays with Daniel while Mom and Dad go see the doctor.

Daniel is excited to meet the new baby. He's going to miss Mom and Dad while they're gone, but he's happy that Grandpere is here to stay with him.

While Daniel and Grandpere wait, Daniel tries to find something special he can give the new baby. He sees an old book at the bottom of his bookshelf called *Margaret's Music*.

That was Daniel's favorite book when he was a baby! He thinks the new baby will like it, too.

Finally, Mr. McFeely comes to tell Daniel that the new baby is here! Grr-ific! Grandpere and Daniel go to Dr. Anna's to visit Mom and Dad Tiger.

Dad Tiger greets Daniel and Grandpere at the door. He takes Daniel in to see Mom Tiger.

Mom hugs Daniel and says, "I love you, Daniel Tiger!"

Daniel hugs her back and says, "I love you!"

Mom asks, "Do you want to meet your baby sister?" Daniel nods his head excitedly.

Daniel is so happy to meet his new sister. He smiles at the baby. She has the cutest little baby nose and the sweetest little baby ears!

"Hi, baby sister. I'm your big brother, Daniel," he says. The baby looks right at Daniel and puts her paw on his paw. Daniel squeals, "She's touching my paw, look!"

Daniel says that he brought a special present for the baby. He takes out *Margaret's Music* and shows it to Mom and Dad.

"Margaret is a lovely name," says Mom.

Grandpere agrees. "It was my mother's name."

"Are you thinking what I'm thinking?" Dad asks. "Margaret is a perfect name for our baby!"

Hurray! Daniel helped name his baby sister.

Daniel wants to give Margaret the book, but the baby starts to cry.
"Why is Margaret crying?" Daniel asks Mom.
"Maybe she's hungry," says Mom. "I'm going to feed her."
Daniel decides to give his present to Margaret later.

It's time to take Baby Margaret home in her stroller. Daniel helps Mom push her through the neighborhood and introduce her to all the neighbors.

"She's so sweet!" says Baker Aker.

"She is music to my ears!" says Music Man Stan.

O the Owl has only seen a baby in a book! Prince Wednesday thinks she is royally little. Katerina thinks she is sooo cute, meow meow! And Miss Elaina is so excited she does a cartwheel.

When they get home, Baby Margaret starts to cry again. Daniel helps Mom change Margaret's diaper.

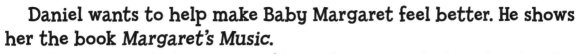

Daniel wants to help make Baby Margaret feel better. He shows her the book *Margaret's Music*.

Baby Margaret stops crying! Daniel is proud to be a big brother—and a big helper.